Dear Pa

Congratulations
the first steps o
The destination

STEP INTO READING® will help your child get there. The program offers five steps to reading success. Each step includes fun stories and colorful art. There are also Step into Reading Sticker Books, Step into Reading Math Readers, Step into Reading Write-In Readers, Step into Reading Phonics Readers, and Step into Reading Phonics First Steps! Boxed Sets—a complete literacy program with something for every child.

Learning to Read, Step by Step!

Ready to Read Preschool–Kindergarten
• big type and easy words • rhyme and rhythm • picture clues
For children who know the alphabet and are eager to begin reading.

Reading with Help Preschool–Grade 1
• basic vocabulary • short sentences • simple stories
For children who recognize familiar words and sound out new words with help.

Reading on Your Own Grades 1–3
• engaging characters • easy-to-follow plots • popular topics
For children who are ready to read on their own.

Reading Paragraphs Grades 2–3
• challenging vocabulary • short paragraphs • exciting stories
For newly independent readers who read simple sentences with confidence.

Ready for Chapters Grades 2–4
• chapters • longer paragraphs • full-color art
For children who want to take the plunge into chapter books but still like colorful pictures.

STEP INTO READING® is designed to give every child a successful reading experience. The grade levels are only guides. Children can progress through the steps at their own speed, developing confidence in their reading, no matter what their grade.

Remember, a lifetime love of reading starts with a single step!

For my favorite little monsters,
Jack and Nathan
—S.C.

For Andrew—
my little monster
—W.T.

Text copyright © 2009 by Shana Corey
Illustrations copyright © 2009 by Will Terry

Visit us on the Web!
www.stepintoreading.com

Educators and librarians, for a variety of teaching tools, visit us at
www.randomhouse.com/teachers

Library of Congress Cataloging-in-Publication Data
Corey, Shana.
Monster parade / by Shana Corey ; illustrated by Will Terry. — 1st ed.
   p. cm. — (Step into reading. A step 2 book)
Summary: Children dressed in monster costumes attend a community party, march in a
Halloween parade, and go trick-or-treating.
ISBN 978-0-375-85638-9 (trade pbk.) — ISBN 978-0-375-95638-6 (lib. bdg.)
[1. Stories in rhyme. 2. Halloween—Fiction. 3. Monsters—Fiction.] I. Terry, Will, ill. II. Title.
PZ8.3.C8183Mo 2009 [E]—dc22 2008009718

Printed in the United States of America   First Edition   10 9 8 7 6 5 4

STEP INTO READING® · STEP 2

Monster Parade

A STICKER READER

by Shana Corey
illustrated by Will Terry

Random House 🏠 New York

The air outside
is cold.
The leaves are
turning gold.

"Hooray! Hooray!"
the children say.
It's Halloween
today!

Time for pumpkins!

Time for treats!

Time for costumes!

Time for sweets!

Time to sing and
time to shout!
Time for monsters
to come out!

Monsters big
and monsters small.
Monsters walk
and monsters crawl.

Monsters marching
two by two.
Monsters marching
right by you!

Silly monsters,

scary monsters,

happy monsters,

hairy monsters.

Furry monsters,

fluffy monsters,

purple monsters,

puffy monsters!

Monsters hungry.

Monsters eat.

Monsters find

a tasty treat!

Monsters munching,

monsters crunching,

monsters chomping,

monsters stomping!

Monsters go from
door to door.
The street's a giant
candy store!

They fill their bags
with more and more.
Then one monster
starts to snore.

Soon another
starts to droop.
She drifts to sleep
on her front stoop.

It is getting
very late.
Monsters try
to stay awake.

Now the moon
is high and bright.
Monsters start
to say good night.

20

Monsters wave
goodbye to friends.
Halloween
is at its end.

Sleepy monsters,
tucked in tight.
Good night, monsters.
Sweet dreams tonight.